# Shooting Star Summer

by CANDICE F. RANSOM · illustrated by KAREN MILONE

CAROLINE HOUSE

BOYDS MILLS PRESS

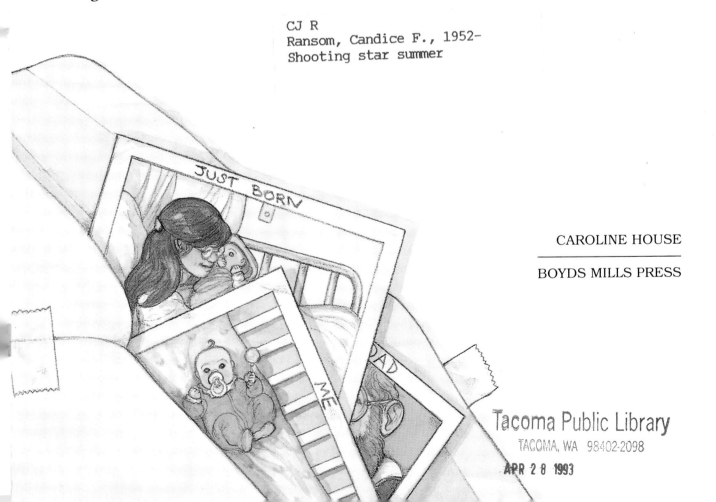

Text copyright © 1992 by Candice Ransom
Illustrations copyright © 1992 by Karen Milone
Published by Caroline House • Boyds Mills Press, Inc.
A Highlights Company • 910 Church Street
Honesdale, Pennsylvania 18431

Publisher Cataloging-in-Publication Data
Ransom, Candice.
Shooting star summer / by Candice Ransom ;
illustrated by Karen Milone.—1st ed.   [32] p. : col. ill. ; cm.
Summary: Apprehensions about a two-week visit
from a cousin are replaced by friendship
and sharing together.
ISBN 1-56397-005-8
[1. Friendship—Fiction.] I. Milone, Karen, ill. II. Title.
[E]—dc20        1992
Library of Congress Catalog Card Number: 91-77621

First edition, 1992
Book designed by Alice Lee Groton
The text of this book is set in 14-point Bookman.
The illustrations are watercolors.
Distributed by St. Martin's Press
Printed in the United States of America

10 9 8 7 6 5 4 3 2 1

For Susan,
in memory of those summers at Grandma's
— C.F.R.

For Miss Katherine Elizabeth Britton
—K.M.

Shannon

me

Shannon age 5

me age 5

My cousin Shannon was coming to visit
for two whole weeks.
She lived in Michigan.
When she was little, Shannon won a baby contest
for her dimples.
And she was the star of her kindergarten play.

"Where will Shannon sleep?" I asked my mom.
"In your room," she answered.
"You two can take turns sleeping on the cot."
I didn't think that was such a great idea.

The day Shannon arrived,
I hid in the persimmon tree.

But nobody missed me, so I finally went into the house.
Shannon had her suitcase open on my bed—
filled with frilly dresses.
Dresses in the summer! I couldn't believe it.

My room seemed awfully crowded with Shannon in it.
"That's my bed," I said.
She didn't answer.
I knew she wouldn't be any fun.

That night while I watched TV,
Shannon read a book.
It looked interesting,
but I didn't ask her what it was about.

After we turned the lights off,
I plumped my pillow and looked out the window.
In the sky I could see the handle of the Big Dipper.
I heard Shannon moving around on her cot.
"Are you crying?" I asked.
Only babies cry at night.
"No," she sniffed. "I just have allergies."
It sure sounded like crying to me.

The next morning
I got up before Shannon
and went outside.
I climbed into my tree house,
but soon she followed me.
That day she was wearing a red dress.
"You'll get dirty," I told her.
A bird as red as Shannon's dress flew by.
"Hey, look, a cardinal," she said.
I wondered if the bird liked Shannon's dress.

The next day it was too hot to do much of anything.
I plopped down on the bottom porch step.
Shannon sat beside me. That day her dress was pink.

"Want to make a clover chain?" she asked.
"I used to make those at home."
"Sounds pretty dumb," I said. What a sissy, I thought.
"We could make a really long one," she said.

So all afternoon we picked clover flowers.
Shannon showed me how
to poke holes in the stems with a pin and
then weave the flowers into one long chain.
When we were done,
the chain stretched from the porch to the garage,
past the mailbox, and back to the porch again.
It was the longest clover chain in the world!

That night I plucked fireflies off grapevine leaves.
Shannon was afraid of bugs, so I caught one for her.
The tiny firefly legs tickled her fingers.
Her cupped hands glowed with firefly light.

"What will we do tomorrow?" she asked.
"Oh, lots of things," I told her. "Wear shorts."
We let the fireflies go,
and they drifted into the night, blinking like stars.

The next day we walked in the woods.
I showed Shannon my poplar-branch hobbyhorse.
She showed me how to make it into a pirate ship.
We took turns walking the plank.

Later we tried to catch crayfish in the creek,
and we built a pebble village on the bank.

Mom helped us make fudge after supper.
It was so hot out, the fudge wouldn't set,
so we ate the sticky mess with spoons.

The next day we started a bird-watching club
and held meetings in the tree house.

Shannon spotted a bird first—a baby robin
fallen from its nest.
"Let's take it home," I said.
"No," said Shannon. "Its mother might miss it."

She knew exactly how to pick up the bird,
cradling it in the folds of her skirt.
She put it under a bush, where its mother
would hear it peeping and come feed it.
I guess a dress can be handy sometimes.

Two weeks went by, and suddenly it was time
for Shannon to go home.
The night before she left,
it was my turn to sleep on the cot.
The cot was lower than my bed, and
I could see more stars out the window—
almost the whole Big Dipper.

"Shannon, look!"
Together we watched a star fall out of the sky,
like the baby robin before it could fly.
The star dropped into our backyard.
"Maybe we'll find it tomorrow," Shannon said.

But the next day Shannon's mother came.
I climbed into the persimmon tree and waved good-bye.
"See you next summer," she called.

That night my room seemed empty
with the cot put away.
I thought about the next day.
Maybe I would play at the creek
or make a clover chain,
but those things wouldn't be much fun
without Shannon.

Then I remembered that Shannon would be back next summer.
We could have our bird-watching club again.
We might even find our baby robin all grown up.

And one year maybe I can visit Shannon in Michigan
and see the Big Dipper from her window.
I'll bet her mom has a cot, too.

To Shannon, love, Me

See you next year!

But I won't wear any dresses!